Dear Parent:
Your child's love of reading starts here!

Every child learns to read in a different way and at his or her own speed. Some go back and forth between reading levels and read favorite books again and again. Others read through each level in order. You can help your young reader improve and become more confident by encouraging his or her own interests and abilities. From books your child reads with you to the first books he or she reads alone, there are I Can Read Books for every stage of reading:

SHARED READING
Basic language, word repetition, and whimsical illustrations, ideal for sharing with your emergent reader

BEGINNING READING
Short sentences, familiar words, and simple concepts for children eager to read on their own

READING WITH HELP
Engaging stories, longer sentences, and language play for developing readers

READING ALONE
Complex plots, challenging vocabulary, and high-interest topics for the independent reader

ADVANCED READING
Short paragraphs, chapters, and exciting themes for the perfect bridge to chapter books

I Can Read Books have introduced children to the joy of reading since 1957. Featuring award-winning authors and illustrators and a fabulous cast of beloved characters, I Can Read Books set the standard for beginning readers.

A lifetime of discovery begins with the magical words "I Can Read!"

Visit www.icanread.com for information
on enriching your child's reading experience.

For all families,
each of which
has its own special history
—J.O'C.

For my grandpa Philip Splaver,
who made his way to America
from Russia when he was just a boy
—R.P.G.

For my grandpas,
both gone before I got here
—T.E.

I Can Read Book® is a trademark of HarperCollins Publishers.

Fancy Nancy: My Family History Text copyright © 2010 by Jane O'Connor Illustrations copyright © 2010 by Robin Preiss Glasser All rights reserved. Printed in the United States of America. No part of this book may be used or reproduced in any manner whatsoever without written permission except in the case of brief quotations embodied in critical articles and reviews. For information address HarperCollins Children's Books, a division of HarperCollins Publishers, 10 East 53rd Street, New York, NY 10022. www.icanread.com

Library of Congress Cataloging-in-Publication Data is available.
ISBN 978-0-06-188270-8 (trade bdg.) — ISBN 978-0-06-188271-5 (pbk.)

14 15 16 17 18   LP/WOR   10   ❖   First Edition

Fancy NANCY

My Family History

by Jane O'Connor

cover illustration by Robin Preiss Glasser

interior illustrations by Ted Enik

HARPER

An Imprint of HarperCollinsPublishers

Do you know about your ancestors?

They are people in your family

who lived long ago.

(You say it like this: ANN-sess-terz.)

Isn't that a great fancy word?

We are writing

ancestor reports in class.

Bree is writing about

her great-grandfather.

He is ninety.

He was a war hero.

Robert's great-grandmother
is one hundred!
She came to America on a ship.
It almost sank.

"You are both lucky,"

I tell my friends.

"You know your ancestors.

All of mine are deceased.

That's fancy for dead."

That night my grandpa calls.

He is coming to visit soon.

His parents are

my great-grandparents.

So I ask, "Were they famous?

Did they have adventures?"

Grandpa says no.

"They were nice, ordinary people."

Ordinary?

That's like plain.

I wish I had fancy ancestors.

Later that night,
Grandpa sends a photo
of my great-grandfather.

Grandpa's email says,

"My dad was kind and honest.

He only lost his temper once.

I broke a teapot

and blamed my sister.

My dad wasn't upset about the teapot.

He was upset that I lied."

"Your dad sounds like
a very lovely person," I reply.
(Reply is fancy for answer.)
"I am going to write
my report about him."

I gather facts from Grandpa.

My ancestor had five children.

He was a bank guard.

He liked to fish.

He lived to be seventy-four.

The next day I illustrate the cover.

(Illustrate is fancy

for making a picture.)

Then I start writing my report.

It begins, "My great-grandpa

was a bank guard."

Hmmm. That does not sound exciting.

So I add something extra.

"Once he stopped a bunch
of bank robbers."

Yes! That sounds very exciting.

Next I write,

"My great-grandpa loved to fish."

Then I add some more exciting stuff.

"One time he caught a shark!"

19

The next day

Clara and Yoko

both read their reports.

I do not mean to brag,

but mine is way more interesting.

After school, I tell my parents,

"On Friday I get to read my report!"

My dad says, "Great!

Grandpa is coming on Thursday.

He can go to school with you.

He is so proud that your report

is about his dad."

I forgot about Grandpa coming.

All of a sudden,

my tummy feels funny.

"I don't think

he is allowed to come,"

I say.

My mom looks at me.

"Of course he can come.

Don't you want him to come?"

Upstairs

I show Mom my report.

"I wanted it to be interesting,

so I exaggerated."

(Exaggerate is a fancy word

for stretching the truth.)

"Honey," Mom says,
"you didn't just exaggerate.
You made up stuff.
That's lying."

I remember the story
about the broken teapot.
My ancestor would be
very upset with me.
My grandpa will be too.

By the time Grandpa comes,

I have written a new report.

This time I stick to the plain truth.

I write about the teapot.

It is an ordinary story.

But I really like it.

On Friday

Grandpa comes to school.

He has brought his dad's top hat.

It's a real one,

not like the one in my magic set.

"My great-grandpa
loved to get dressed up,"
I tell everyone.
"I must get being fancy from him!"

Fancy Nancy's Fancy Words

These are the fancy words in this book:

Ancestors—people in your family who lived long ago (you say it like this: ANN-sess-terz)

Deceased—dead

Exaggerate—stretch the truth

Illustrate—make a picture

Ordinary—plain

Reply—answer